The Boxcar Children investigate legendary creatures!

The Aldens grabbed their bags and headed to their campsite with their new tentmates, Toby and Tara.

"West Camp is right below Sasquatch Ridge!" said Toby. "We will see a bigfoot for sure!"

"Bigfoot?" Violet asked. "I thought we came to Camp Quest to look for fossils. Is that another name for a dinosaur?"

Toby shook his head. "I'm talking about creatures from the *present*. You know—Bigfoot! The hairy apelike creature. This whole area is nicknamed Bigfoot Valley because so many people have seen bigfoots here."

"I knew there were things hiding in these woods!" Benny said.

Violet wasn't so sure. She had read stories about creatures like Bigfoot. But those stories weren't true, were they?

THE BOXCAR CHILDREN®

CREATED BY
GERTRUDE CHANDLER WARNER

BOOK 1

THE SECRET OF BIGFOOT VALLEY

ALBERT WHITMAN & COMPANY
CHICAGO, ILLINOIS

Printed in the United States of America
10 9 8 7 6 5 4 3 2 1 LB 24 23 22 21 20

Illustrations by Thomas Girard

Visit The Boxcar Children® online at www.boxcarchildren.com.
For more information about Albert Whitman & Company,
visit our website at www.albertwhitman.com.

CONTENTS

CREATURES FROM THE PAST

"Do you think there might be one out there?" Benny Alden asked.

Jessie looked past her little brother out the car window. Outside, the forest was thick and dark. "One what?"

"A dinosaur!" said Benny. "A real, live one."

Henry turned around from the passenger seat. He was the oldest of the four Alden children and was helping Grandfather navigate. "We're going to summer camp to look for dinosaur *bones*," he said. "Real dinosaurs don't exist anymore, remember?"

"I know that." Benny crossed his arms. He was still learning to read, but for weeks Jessie had been helping him memorize the names of dinosaurs, when they lived, and what they liked to eat. His favorite was a single-horned plant eater called Monoclonius.

"Still, what if there's still one out there?" Benny continued. "If *I* was a Monoclonius, this is where I would live. No pesky humans, and all the food you could ever eat!"

"Even dinosaur Benny thinks about food all the time," Violet said with a giggle.

Violet shared Benny's imagination. But she was thinking more about the kinds of pictures she could take of the Colorado scenery than about seeing dinosaurs. She added, "Don't worry, Benny. If there's one out here, I'll get a picture for you."

At a sign for Camp Quest, Grandfather slowed the car and pulled onto a dirt road. Before long the Aldens pulled into a grassy parking lot. The lot was full of families unloading sleeping bags, duffels, and backpacks from their cars.

It had been a long drive from the airport in Denver. All of the Aldens were excited to get out and stretch. As soon as Grandfather parked, Benny opened his door and ran to the edge of the forest. He got on all fours and made a grunting sound he imagined a Monoclonius would make.

A young woman dressed in a red T-shirt came over to the Aldens' rental car. She looked them over. Then she wound a pen through her springy hair as she studied a clipboard. "You must be…the Alden family?" she said.

"Good guess!" said Henry. "How'd you know?"

The young woman pointed the pen at her clipboard. "Let's see: Four children who look like they are from the same family. Two boys, ages six and fourteen, and two girls, ages ten and twelve…" She looked up and smiled. "That's what we do here at Camp Quest. We follow where the evidence leads."

Benny ran back to the car, still on all fours.

"And you must be Benny," the young woman said.

"I think he's a Monoclonius right now," Jessie laughed.

"Well, my name is Michelle, and I'm one of the counselors here. We divide campers between four sites: North, South, East, and West. You four will be staying in West Camp—with me!"

A van pulled up nearby, and more campers began to pile out. "Well, it's nice to meet you, Aldens," Michelle said. "I'll be back in a little bit. As soon as we've got everyone checked in, we can head to our campsite."

As Michelle hurried off, a small brown dog with a bandanna around its neck ran up. The dog put its paws up on Henry's leg and let out a little bark. Behind the dog was a woman about Grandfather's age. She had long, silvery-black hair and wore a gold necklace.

"Welcome, Aldens!" the woman said.

"You know our name too?" Benny said, standing up.

Grandfather gave the woman a hug. "Children, this is Dr. Iris Perez, the camp director. She's an old friend of mine."

"You can call me Dr. Iris," the woman said. "Everyone does. I'm so happy to finally meet you! Your grandfather wrote me that you children love adventures. He even told me about your boxcar clubhouse—how very resourceful!"

"We like being outside," Jessie said. She turned to Benny, who was back to running along the edge of the forest. "As you can see."

"You sound just like your grandfather when he was young," said Dr. Iris. "Would you believe he and I hunted fossils together when we were your age? Our fathers were friends, you see, and we met up during the summer to go camping together. We had a lot of fun."

Grandfather chuckled. "We certainly did. And Iris went on to become a paleontologist. She's still hunting fossils."

The camp director touched the necklace she was

wearing. It had a tiny magnifying glass on the end of a chain. "I still have the gift your grandfather sent me when I got my degree."

At the mention of fossils, Benny had come back to the group. "What is a…a paleo…paleo-something?" he asked.

"Paleontologist," Dr. Iris said. "It's a big word, isn't it?"

Benny nodded. He tried to count the letters with his hands, but he ran out of fingers.

"Once you know what each part of the word means, it won't seem so big," Dr. Iris said. "Paleontologists study fossils, so we can learn about the history of life on Earth. *Paleo* is a Greek word that means *ancient* or *very old*. The next part of the word, *onto*, means *being*. Fossils come from ancient *beings*, you see. And a word that ends in *logy* means the study of something. So a paleontologist is someone who *studies* ancient beings."

"Like a Monoclonius?" Benny asked.

Dr. Iris smiled. "That's quite a big word too," she

6

said. "Yes, we study all creatures from the past."

The little dog gave another bark and nudged his nose at Henry's leg.

"I'm afraid Rex doesn't like to be ignored," said Dr. Iris.

"Is he named for a *Tyrannosaurus rex?*" asked Benny.

"That's exactly right," said Dr. Iris. "I know it's a large name for a little dog, but he doesn't know he's small. This guy would take on a bear if he had the chance."

Michelle came back with two campers, a boy and a girl, each with curly hair and freckles. The girl was looking at her phone. The boy had a big map in his hands.

"Aldens, meet your tentmates," Michelle said.

"Nice to meet you," the boy said. "I'm Toby Payne. And this is my sister, Tara." The girl nodded but did not look up from her phone.

"Toby, you will be with Henry and Benny," Michelle said. "And, Tara, you are with their sisters, Jessie and Violet." She took a stack of maps from her clipboard. "Now, see if you can find your way to West Camp using your maps. You can show your parents and grandparents where you'll be staying. Then it will be time for good-byes."

The children grabbed their bags and followed the maps toward West Camp. Behind them, Dr. Iris walked with Grandfather and Toby and Tara's dad.

"West Camp is right below Sasquatch Ridge!" said Toby. "We will see a bigfoot for sure!"

"Bigfoot?" Violet asked. "I thought we came here to look for fossils. Is that another name for a dinosaur?"

Toby shook his head. "I'm talking about creatures from the *present*. You know—Bigfoot! The hairy apelike creature. This whole area is nicknamed Bigfoot Valley because so many people have seen bigfoots here."

"Really?" said Benny. "I knew there were things hiding in these woods!"

Violet had read stories about creatures like Bigfoot. But she didn't think they were real. "Are there really bigfeet here?" she asked Michelle.

"Bigfoots," Toby corrected.

Michelle shook her head. "Remember, at Camp Quest we look at the evidence. I have never seen evidence of any bigfoots." She smiled. "Or bigfeet."

Toby crossed his arms. "Just because you haven't seen it doesn't mean it's not real," he said. "I'm going to find one this week and prove it's real!"

Toby took off running to the campsite. "Last one there's a rotten egg!" he called.

The Aldens took their time, walking slowly with Michelle and Tara. When they arrived at West Camp, there was a young man about Michelle's age standing outside the tents. He didn't notice them at first. He was too busy spraying bug spray and swatting at insects.

Michelle cleared her throat. "This is Jared," she said. "The other counselor here at West Camp." She turned to Jared. "Did a curly-haired boy already arrive? He ran ahead."

"Oh, hi. Yes, you can put your things in those two tents there. Toby went straight into the one on the right." Jared continued to swat at bugs. He did not look comfortable. He had pale skin, but his face and arms were sunburned. "I don't blame him," Jared continued. "These bugs are terrible!"

The children thanked Jared and headed to their tents. Violet and Jessie set about laying out their sleeping bags and other belongings. Their tent was nice and big, and it was nestled under a tree among the other tents in West Camp. Before long the little place felt like home.

Violet wanted to talk with her new tentmate, Tara. But she seemed like she was only interested in her phone. She did not even unpack. So as Jessie tidied up, Violet lay back on her sleeping bag and went through the pictures on her camera.

Looking at pictures was a nice distraction. She had not minded when Benny talked about dinosaurs roaming the wilderness. She knew that was impossible, but she did not expect to hear about strange creatures living in the forest. Could the stories Toby heard be true?

Suddenly, there was a commotion outside. A dog was barking loudly. Then Violet heard Dr. Iris yell, "Rex, come back!"

CHAPTER 2

LEGENDS OF
THE VALLEY

The girls hurried out their tent. Rex was running toward the woods, and Dr. Iris was running after him. The boys were already outside, watching with Grandfather.

"Heel!" Dr. Iris called. She had to yell twice more before the dog finally stopped at the edge of the forest. Rex continued to growl, so she bent down and picked him up.

"Did he see a squirrel?" Benny asked. "Watch

loves to chase squirrels." Watch was the children's wirehaired terrier. They'd had to leave him at home for their trip to summer camp.

"No. He doesn't act like that around squirrels, or any other of the animals that live in these woods," said Dr. Iris. She looked worried. "He chased a raccoon once that was trying to get into the dumpster, but only until it ran into the woods. He thinks the camp is his property and the woods are theirs. I haven't seen him like this before."

"There's *something* in the woods he doesn't like," Violet said.

Toby pushed aside some branches and peered into the forest. "I don't see anything. Can I go look?"

"No!" said their counselor Jared. He was now wearing a mosquito net around his head. "You might get lost! And there are more insects in there than out here. Bugs, animals, all sorts of things!"

Dr. Iris's cell phone rang. She answered it and listened for a few seconds. "Okay, I'll be there in a moment." When she hung up, she said, "I've got to run. The cook's helper called in sick. There are supplies to unload. And it seems like a good time to get Rex away from here."

"We can help unload too," said Henry.

Jessie and Violet nodded.

"That would be wonderful!" said Dr. Iris. "You should have enough time before we start the camp scavenger hunt." She turned to Grandfather. "James, are your grandchildren always so helpful?"

Grandfather chuckled. "You should see them when there is a mystery to solve," he said.

Toby and Benny were still peering into the woods, and Tara was nearby, looking for service on her phone.

"All right, children, you will have plenty of time to explore later," Dr. Iris said. "And, Tara, since you are officially at camp now, it's time to put away your phone. If I see it again, I will have to put it in my office. Remember, everyone at camp agreed to go a week without electronics?"

Tara sighed but put the phone in her pocket.

Violet held up her digital camera. "Is this okay?" she asked. She had read the rule about no electronics online, but she didn't think it might include her camera.

Dr. Iris looked unsure. "Yes, okay, you may hold on to your camera. But only use it during free time. We have lots of important work to do this week."

"Well, it sounds like it's time for me to get out of your way," Grandfather said. "But I'll be back to pick you up in a week. Benny, I expect to hear all about your Monoclonius findings when you're done."

Benny stood up straight and saluted. "Aye-aye!" he said. Then he gave Grandfather a big hug.

After everyone had said their good-byes, the children followed Dr. Iris through the camp to a large wooden building. "This is our main lodge," she explained. "The dining hall is on one side, and the activity rooms and offices are on the other."

She led them to the back of the lodge, where a man was taking a crate of apples out of the back of a truck. The man wore a chef's apron. He was bald and had a camp bandanna tied around his head. Behind him was a skinny teenage boy in a plaid shirt and baseball cap. The boy walked through the kitchen door carrying a heavy sack of food.

"I've found you some more helpers, Chef Peplinkski," Dr. Iris said.

After everyone was introduced, she explained that she needed to leave so she could go greet more campers. "When you are finished, go around to the front of the lodge. That's where we're meeting to start the scavenger hunt."

"Happy to meet you!" the man said after Dr. Iris had left. "Just call me Chef Pepper. It's easier to remember than Peplinkski. It's been my nickname since I first set foot in a kitchen."

"Jessie, you're always cooking at home. You should have a nickname!" said Benny. He thought a moment. "If I had a nickname, it would be Chef Blueberry." Benny licked his lips. "Or maybe Chef Pancakes."

Henry laughed. "Benny, those are just your favorite foods," he said.

"Well, Chef Blueberry Pancake," Chef Pepper said with a chuckle. "If you want to work in the kitchen, you can start by helping me get these boxes into the pantry."

The boy in the plaid shirt hurried back out the door, nearly running into Chef Pepper. "Len, watch where you are going!" the chef said.

The boy threw up his hands. "Sorry, Pep. I'm in a hurry. That's what happens when you have two jobs. My dad is expecting me back at the office soon."

"Okay, okay," the chef said. "Everyone, this is Len. He helps me out. He also works at the weekly newspaper in town."

The children introduced themselves to Len and began moving the boxes into the pantry. It didn't take long with everyone helping. Jessie and Tara each took one side of the last crate and carried it in. "Many hands make like work," Chef Pepper said. "You can put that here," he added, pointing to an empty spot on a shelf.

As Jessie set the box on the shelf, she noticed

another room next to the pantry. It was full of plates and silverware and serving pans. "Look at all these kitchen supplies," she said to Tara. "A whole room full of them."

Tara went inside and looked around. For the first time, she seemed interested in something other than her phone. She even knelt down to look at the lower shelves.

"It takes a lot of effort and supplies to feed a bunch of hungry campers," said Chef Pepper. "Some campers volunteer for Kitchen Patrol, if you are interested."

Jessie looked at Tara. Maybe Kitchen Patrol could be something they did as tentmates. "What do you think?" she asked.

But Tara just shrugged. "I don't think so."

"Well, the van is empty," Len said as he came back into the pantry with a piece of paper. "Here's the delivery order for you to sign, Pep."

The chef signed the paper and handed it back to him. "We'll see you on Monday. I know you are busy, but try to be on time then. If you don't get here in the morning, it throws off my whole day."

"I'll try, but I'm working at the newspaper office that day too. Oh, I nearly forgot. My dad wants to know if you have any story tips he can write about. Any big fossil finds? Whole dinosaurs?"

Benny's eyes got wide. "Has someone found a whole dinosaur before?" he asked.

"Not a camper," the chef said. "Though some have been found in the area."

"We read that the state fossil of Colorado was the stegosaurus," Henry said. "So maybe someday a camper will find one of those."

"How can a dinosaur be the state fossil?" Tara asked. "I thought fossils were from little sea creatures."

"Some fossils are from sea creatures, but dinosaur bones are fossils too," Henry said. "The bones have been changed over millions of years into something more like rocks."

"That's right," said Chef Pepper. "Campers have found some excellent dinosaur footprints and bones, but not a whole dinosaur. That would be a rare discovery. Len, you can tell your father we are having a fantastic camp year, just like always. He'll have to look somewhere else for tips."

"Do you ever get tips about Bigfoot?" Toby asked.

"Actually," said Len, "that was going to be my next question." He pulled out a poster showing a hairy sheepdog. "Have you heard anything about this dog that went missing, Pep?"

Chef Pepper looked at the photo but shook his head. "I'm afraid not. What does a missing dog have to do with Bigfoot?"

"The dog's owners were hiking through the valley," said Len, "when they heard a noise in the woods, and the dog ran after it. They searched for hours but couldn't find the poor fellow. Some people around town are saying a bigfoot got it."

"That's terrible," said Violet. "Has anyone seen a bigfoot here?"

Len shrugged. "Hard to say. A few times a year, people think they see something in the woods. We usually don't report it unless they take a picture, but the pictures are never very clear. We have bears around here too, so it's hard to tell if the photos are of bears or something else."

"Well, I think that's enough talk of imaginary beasts," Chef Pepper said. "Off you go now, so I can get to work."

The children said good-bye to Chef Pepper and headed to the front of the main lodge. Groups from all four camps were gathering for the scavenger hunt.

"Welcome, campers!" Dr. Iris said. "We're going to have you get to know Camp Quest with a scavenger hunt! As you find each place on the list, a counselor will make a stamp on your map. When you've got them all stamped, meet back here. Stay with your tentmates. We operate on the buddy system here. No one goes off by themselves. That way no one gets lost or gets hurt and can't get help."

Toby raised his hand.

"Yes?" Dr. Iris said.

"Is there a prize for the first one back?"

Dr. Iris laughed. "No, it's not a competition. The purpose is to get to know the camp. You can go at your own pace."

As soon Michelle and Jared handed out the list of clues, Toby took off running toward one of the other campsites. Henry and Benny ran to catch up.

"I guess Toby's pace is fast." Jessie chuckled.

"Your brother seems competitive," Violet said to Tara.

"He is," said Tara. As the girls moved away from the rest of the group, she took out her phone again. "He's always trying to be the center of attention."

"Well, scavenger hunts are more about brains than speed," said Jessie. She read the first clue. It was a riddle:

I dive from the ridge far above.
Look up, and you'll see the setting sun.

"Hmm…" said Violet. "I wonder what that means."

Jessie turned to her map. "It looks like each of the four campsites is named after a different bird. There's Cardinal, Hummingbird, Falcon, and Kingfisher."

"The clue says the bird dives from high up," said Violet. "Cardinals and hummingbirds don't do that, do they?"

"Good point," said Jessie. "That leaves Kingfisher, which is East Camp, and Falcon, which is West Camp."

"What do you think the second part of the clue means?" Violet asked. "Does it mean the bird is colorful like the sun? I don't know about kingfishers, but falcons aren't very colorful."

"Kingfishers sometimes have yellow on them," said Tara, looking up from her phone. "But I think they're blue."

"Maybe it doesn't have to do with the color of the birds." Jessie turned the map in her hands. "It might just be talking about the actual sun."

"The sun rises in the east and sets in the west," said Violet. "So it must be leading us…that way!"

The girls set off toward the ridge that rose up

beyond West Camp. Jessie and Violet led the way. Tara trailed behind.

As they passed the campsite and headed up the path toward the ridge, Violet said, "Tara, didn't your brother say this place was nicknamed Sasquatch Ridge?"

When Tara didn't answer, Violet thought it was because she was on her phone. After all, she had barely looked up from it since they had arrived. But when Violet looked back, Tara was nowhere to be found!

"Uh, Jessie," Violet said. "Where did Tara go?"

"I don't know," said Jessie. "I thought she was right behind us!"

A DAY FULL OF STRANGENESS

D o you think she went off the trail?" Violet asked. "Should we go looking for her?"

Jessie peered into the forest. The sun was still above the ridge, but under the trees, it was already starting to get dark. "Let's head back to the main lodge and find Dr. Iris," she said. "She'll know what to do."

As the girls backtracked, they called out Tara's name, but there was no answer. They passed other groups of campers heading to West Camp. Finally, Jessie and Violet saw a face they recognized.

"Tara!" Jessie called as her tentmate came up the trail. "Are you okay?"

"Of course," Tara said. "Why?"

"We were worried about you," said Violet. "We thought you got lost. Where did you go?"

"Sorry," said Tara. "It just seemed like you two had the scavenger hunt taken care of. I wanted to go check out the insides of some of the buildings."

Jessie and Violet looked at each other in surprise. They knew she wasn't interested in the scavenger hunt. But what could be so important that she would go off without telling them?

—

By the end of the scavenger hunt, Benny's stomach was rumbling. Henry, Benny, and Toby had run all around camp to try to finish first, but a team from North Camp had just beaten them. Now all Benny could think about was food—even more than usual.

"Here's our table," Henry called after they'd filled their plates in the dining hall. The West campers' tables were all set up in a row. Each one had a cutout of a falcon in the center.

Benny licked his lips at the big pile of spaghetti on his plate. But as he was about to dig in, Michelle stood up from the front of the tables. "West campers, before you start eating, we counselors want to welcome you and tell you a little about ourselves now. Jared, why don't you go first?"

Benny sighed and put down his fork.

"Well, there's not that much to tell," Jared said, standing up. "I'm studying paleontology in college, and this is my first year as a counselor." He sat back down.

As Jared sat back down, Jessie whispered, "He doesn't seem too excited to be here."

"Maybe he's just hungry," Benny said, picking up his fork.

But before Benny could start eating, Michelle

stood back up. "Okay, then. Well, Jared is a person of few words, but I'm not!"

Benny huffed. He put down his fork once more.

Michelle told the campers all about herself and her family and what she was studying in college. "I came to this camp as a camper and loved it so much I wanted to come back and be a counselor," she said. "This is my fourth year counseling."

"Have you ever seen a bigfoot around camp?" a camper asked. "We read stories in the local newspaper about them."

Michelle laughed. "As I've said to others, those are just rumors. I haven't even seen a bear. We make so much noise with our singalongs and games, creatures avoid us."

Finally, the children dug in as Michelle continued chatting with campers. Jared hardly said another word. As they were finishing the main course, he stood up and said, "I don't feel well. I need to go lie down in the nurse's office."

"Oh, I can call the nurse," said Michelle, glancing

around the dining hall. "It looks like she's already gone to her cabin, but she'll come right back."

"No, I don't want to bother her," said Jared. "I get these headaches once in a while, and I just need to stay in a dark room."

Jared didn't come back to the table, even for dessert. When everyone was done, the campers walked back to West Camp without him.

At the campground, Michelle started a fire in the fire ring, and the campers down sat on logs in a circle around it. As it got dark, they roasted s'mores and talked about what they were most excited about for the week.

They were just about to sing songs and play a game when Rex ran up. The dog flopped down by Violet as Dr. Iris walked up. She raised her hand to get everyone's attention. "Before I turn in for the night, I just want to remind you about a few rules," she said. "Remember, no phones. We want you to have fun in a different way than you do at home. Also, no food in the tents. We don't want to attract any wildlife. They have plenty of their own food in the woods. So if anyone brought snacks, now is the time to go get them and give them to me. I'll keep them in the office, and you can have them back when camp is over. Anyone have anything?"

No one raised a hand.

"Okay then, good," she said. "Tomorrow, we'll get together after breakfast and go over the right techniques for fossil hunting. Then, after lunch, we'll be off to hunt for real fossils! I am going to check in with the other campsites now. I will see you in the morning!"

Dr. Iris began to walk away, but Rex didn't move from his spot by Violet.

"Does Rex get to stay with us all night?" Benny asked.

"No," Michelle said. "Rex likes West Camp for some reason. I'm not sure why, but he stays here until Dr. Iris whistles for him. Then he goes home to her cabin."

Rex thumped his tail as if he knew they were talking about him.

"Now, how about a song?" said Michelle.

The children sang two songs in rounds. Tara and Toby competed to see who could sing louder. When they started the third song, Violet noticed Rex raise his head and sniff the air. She thought maybe Dr. Iris had whistled and she hadn't heard it because of the songs. But then she saw that Rex was looking toward the trees, not the camp buildings.

The dog let out a low growl. No one else noticed, but when Violet saw the hair on the back of the dog's neck rise, she said out loud, "Look at Rex."

The dog took a step toward the woods.

As Michelle stopped singing, the other campers began noticing the dog. It grew so quiet the only sound was the crackling of the fire. An owl hooted in the distance.

"I hear something," Benny said.

A branch snapped, and then there was a rustling sound as if something was moving through the forest. Everyone held very still.

Suddenly, there was a horrible screeching noise.

It sounded like it was just feet away. A camper screamed, and then came the sound of more branches breaking. Rex took off running toward the woods, barking wildly.

"Rex! Rex! Come back!" Michelle yelled as she ran after him. "Everyone stay here."

"It might be a bear!" one of the campers cried.

"It might be a bear," Henry said. "One might be attracted by the smell of our s'mores. But a bear isn't going to come up to a campfire with a lot of people sitting around it. We're safe here."

"That's right," Jessie said. "Let's wait for Michelle."

It didn't take long for the counselor to come back with Rex. Violet let out a sigh of relief.

"He didn't go far," Michelle said. "I guess it was a bear, but one has never come close to camp before."

"That screeching noise didn't sound like it came from a bear," said Toby. "I knew there were bigfoots out here!"

Tara shuddered. "It was scary, whatever it was. I want to go home."

"Me too!" another camper said. "Bigfoots are dangerous."

"It wasn't a bigfoot," Michelle said. "I have been coming to this camp for years. They don't exist."

"I bet it comes at night and sneaks around while we are sleeping," said Toby. "That's what I'd do if I was a bigfoot."

"This is not a good time to have a debate about Bigfoot," Michelle said. "Whatever it was, it won't come to the tents for food, because we won't have any food here. Right?"

"Right," Henry said.

"We can play the game now, can't we?" said Jessie, changing the subject.

"Yes! The game. I'd forgotten about the game." The counselor sat back down. She was still holding onto Rex, who kept looking in the direction of the woods. "It's a fun one, so we can get to know each other."

She had to repeat herself because some of the campers were still talking about the noise, but finally everyone quieted down. "Violet, why don't you start?" Michelle said. "Tell us something you like that starts with the letter *A*, and then Jessie will go next. Jessie is going to repeat Violet's name and what Violet likes, then tell us something she likes that starts with the letter *B*. It gets harder with the more things you have to remember, so it's okay if you forget. We'll help."

"I'm good at remembering things!" Toby boasted.

"Then this should be an easy game for you," the counselor said. "Go ahead, Violet."

Violet thought for a moment. "My name is Violet, and I like...art!"

"Good! Now Jessie, can you repeat what Violet just said?"

"Yes, Violet likes art. My name is Jessie, and I like baking."

Tara was sitting by Jessie, so she went next, repeating what Violet and Jessie said. After that, she added, "My name is Tara, and I like computer games." Benny and Henry went next.

Toby was almost last. He started off remembering everything, but he forgot Henry had said he liked eagles. "Wait, don't tell me. I'll remember."

After a few moments, Michelle asked if he'd like help.

"I thought you said you were good at remembering," Tara teased.

"I am! Henry didn't say it loud enough. I didn't hear him! This is a stupid game." Toby got up and stomped away from the fire.

"Don't be such a baby," Tara called after him.

"Let's try to be nice to each other," Michelle said.

Then Benny gave a big yawn, and the counselor said, "Okay, maybe it's best to call it a night. We have a busy day tomorrow."

As the campers were going to their tents, Violet glanced back over her shoulder to see Michelle looking at the woods. "I hope whatever made that noise doesn't come back," Violet told Jessie. "I wish Rex could stay with us, like Watch does."

Violet and Jessie were just settling into their

sleeping bags when another shout came from outside. This time, it was one they recognized.

"That sounds like Benny!" Jessie said, scrambling up and unzipping the tent. She ran out, and the others followed.

"Is it Bigfoot?" someone called out.

"Who screamed?" someone else yelled.

When Jessie, Violet, and Tara got outside, they saw Benny, Henry, and Toby standing outside of their own tent. Jared was running toward them from the lodge path. Other campers crowded around the three boys.

"What happened?" Jessie asked. She went over and put her arm around Benny.

"The tent…the tent is full of spiders!" he cried.

"Toby! You didn't!" Tara marched into the tent and came back out. She held up her hand. It had a big black spider on it. One of the other campers shrieked.

"It's not real," Tara said. "They're all plastic. Toby, you did this, didn't you? You said you weren't going to play pranks."

"I didn't do this!" Toby said. "Why would I put spiders in my own tent?"

"If you didn't do it, then who did?" Tara asked.

For a moment, no one said anything.

"They looked real," Benny said in a quiet voice.

"Some pranks are in good fun. This one was not," Jared said. "No more of this sort of thing. Let's pick them all up so we can go to sleep."

The girls went back to their tent. Jessie and Violet climbed into their sleeping bags. It had been an eventful day, and they were ready for sleep.

Tara rummaged in her backpack and pulled out a phone. She looked at Jessie and Violet. "You won't tell anyone, will you?" she asked. "I know we aren't supposed to have phones here, but my team is counting on me."

"What team?" Violet asked.

"My online computer game team. If I don't play, we can't get enough points. I have to log in every day to check on the village I made in the game. The village will disappear if I don't check

40

on it, and I worked really hard to build it."

Jessie yawned. "We won't tell."

"You could explain to Dr. Iris," said Violet. "Then you won't have to hide the phone."

"She would never understand," Tara said. "My dad doesn't. And it's not fair that the counselors get to use theirs when we don't. I saw Jared checking his when we were getting our plates for dinner. But thanks for not telling. I wasn't sure when I came to camp if I'd meet anyone who would be nice."

"You're welcome," Jessie said, yawning again.

They said goodnight. As Violet lay in her sleeping bag, she noticed that Tara was on her phone for a long time. There was something strange about that. But then again, a lot of strange things had happened that day. Tara had gone missing during the scavenger hunt. Their counselor, Jared, didn't seem to want to be at the camp. There were strange noises in the woods. It had been a day full of strangeness.

Violet was ready for a new one.

FOOD FOR THOUGHT

The next morning everyone was eager to get started. After breakfast, the campers headed to the science rooms, where Dr. Iris talked to them about fossil hunting.

"Fossils are the remains of ancient creatures," she explained. "They can be from plants or animals. They are creatures' bones, shells, teeth, or even footprints. Studying fossils helps us learn about the plants and animals that no one has ever seen. Because we have the fossils, we know they existed." She turned to Michelle. "Why don't you explain where we are going today?"

Michelle walked over to a large map on the wall. "Camp Quest is here," she said, pointing to a spot marked with a circle. She moved her finger to a blue line. "But we are going here, to a streambed."

"Why are we looking for fossils in a stream?" asked Henry.

"Are we looking for water dinosaurs?" said Benny.

"Those are good questions," Dr. Iris said. "After all these years, most fossils are buried under many feet of soil. If we dug down deep enough, even right outside the lodge, we might find some. But think how much work that would be! Can anyone think of how a stream could help us?"

Jessie spoke up. She had learned about erosion in geology class. "The flowing water in the stream takes the soil and washes it away," she said.

"That's right," said Dr. Iris. "The stream does the digging for us! It cuts down to the rock, where the fossils are. As for what kind of fossils we will find, Benny, that is for you to figure out."

When the science session was finished, the campers hurried through lunch and got on a bus to take them to the fossil-hunting site. From the parking lot, it was a short hike to the stream. "It's so pretty here," Violet said. She twirled around. "Look at all the mountains and the trees!"

Toby stared up into the woods. "We're far away from everything," he said. "This is perfect bigfoot territory."

Tara snuck up behind him and grabbed his shoulders. "Boo!" she said.

He jumped and pushed her away. "Stop it!"

"All right, everyone," Michelle said. "Let's remember why we are here. Time to put on your wading shoes and look for fossils! Jared and I have the charts with us. If you find something, come to us, and we'll see if it matches any common fossils."

As soon as Benny had his wading shoes on, he splashed into the stream. "I'm going to find a Monoclonius bone!" he said. "Maybe even a horn!"

Henry chuckled. "Come on, Benny. We can look together."

It was a sunny and hot day, but the water was very cool. "How can the air be so warm, but the water be so cold?" asked Violet as she waded in with Jessie.

"We're not far from the mountains," Jessie said. "The water is coming from snow melting higher up. It feels good, doesn't it?"

Suddenly water splashed on both of them as Benny pulled something large out of the water. "I think I found a dinosaur bone!" he said. "Henry, look!"

The object in Benny's hands was long and pale white. Henry put his hand on Benny's shoulder. "Benny, that's a tree branch without any bark."

"Oh," said Benny. "Whoops." He put the branch back in the water.

"Look at the rocks, Benny," Jessie said. "Try to find ones with interesting shapes."

After a few minutes of searching, Benny picked up something much smaller. "What about this?" he asked. The object was shaped like a seashell. But it was as hard as a rock.

"Let's see," said Henry. The two waded out and brought the object to Michelle. Together, they looked at the pictures on the chart.

"It looks just like this one!" Benny said, pointing to one of the pictures.

"You're right. It does," said Michelle. "That means you found the first one. Everyone, Benny found a brachiopod!"

"A brachio-what?" said Benny. "I don't know that one."

"Brachiopods are like clams and oysters," said Michelle. "They live at the bottom of the sea."

"So this whole place was covered by water once?" Benny said.

Michelle nodded. "It was a warm sea back then."

Benny's eyes got big. He hadn't found his Monoclonius fossil, but it was cool to touch something that had lived at the bottom of the ocean millions of years ago.

Soon, everyone had found at least one fossil. Toby and Tara kept running from place to place, sure they would find a better spot.

"I've got six!" Toby shouted. "How many do you have?"

"Five, but I bet I find more than you before we're done!" she called back.

"It's not a competition," Michelle said. "Scientists work together in teams, and we're a team."

As the afternoon went on, it got even hotter. Jessie and Violet stopped for a break and to get a drink from the cooler in the shade. Jared was there, mopping his forehead with his bandanna. His face was all red.

Jessie poured herself a cup of water and took a big drink. Although it was hot, she was happy to finally be looking for fossils, especially after such a rocky first day. "You're lucky to have such a fun job," she said to Jared. "I'd like to be a camp counselor here when I'm old enough."

Jared frowned. "I was supposed to be working in

a nice air-conditioned history museum this summer," he said. "I was going to be cleaning actual dinosaur bones, not standing out with the sun and the bugs and the who knows what in the woods."

"Why aren't you working at the museum?" Violet asked.

"They were short on counselors," Jared explained, "and they had too many people who wanted the museum job. They took someone with more experience. If camp didn't run so long, I would have been able to take one of the shorter runs, but I can't even do that as long as I'm stuck here."

"Sorry," Jessie said. "I hope you get to do that job next summer."

"I do too," the counselor grumbled. He touched his nose. "Am I getting more sunburned?"

"It is pretty red," said Violet.

Just then one of the other counselors called to him from the stream. Jared sighed, wiped his forehead again, and walked away.

"It's too bad he has to be here if he doesn't want

to be. I thought everyone liked camping." Violet took a drink of water.

"I thought that too," said Jessie. "But between Tara and Jared, I'm having my doubts." Then she brightened up. "Ready to go find some fossils?"

"Let's do it," said Violet. "I can't let Benny find more than me!"

Late in the afternoon, the children headed back to camp. They laid out their fossils on the tables in the science room and started to clean them with brushes.

Dr. Iris walked around and looked at the finds. "We have eight different kinds of fossils. That's a good day's work," she said. "Look them over a little more. The cards next to them are there to help you quiz yourself on the names. When you are done, everyone can get ready for dinner. Tomorrow morning, we'll work on recording information about our findings. We'll measure them and then make a time line of when these creatures lived. Scientists always keep records of what they observe and what they find."

That evening after dinner, everyone headed back

to their campsites to play games. Toby and some of the other campers ran, but since Benny was tired, the Aldens walked together.

Violet craned her neck to look ahead. "Where's Tara?" she asked. "I didn't see her with Toby."

"I don't remember seeing her leave the dining hall," Jessie answered. She turned around to look behind her.

Tara came running down the path. She was wearing her backpack, which bounced as she ran. "I'm coming!" Tara called. Then, when she caught up with them, she said, "I wanted to say hi to Chef Pepper. Let's catch up with everyone else!"

Before Jessie could explain that they were walking slow to stay with Benny, Tara jogged away.

"That's strange," Jessie said. "Tara didn't seem interested in doing Kitchen Patrol before. Why was she visiting Chef Pepper?"

"Maybe she changed her mind," said Violet.

"Maybe," said Jessie. "But why did she have her backpack on?"

"I bet she was trying to get seconds," said Benny.

He rubbed his tummy. "Maybe we should say hi to Chef Pepper after breakfast tomorrow."

The Aldens laughed as they made their way to their campsite. But as they got closer, they heard someone yelling.

"That sounds like Toby," Henry said.

"I'm not so tired now," Benny said. "Let's see what's going on!"

When the Aldens got to West Camp, they saw Toby pointing at the ground. The other campers were gathered around him. "Who did this?" he said. He looked upset.

"Did what?" Henry asked.

"Someone ate all my candy!" said Toby. There were wrappers scattered all over the ground.

Jared and Michelle made her way through the campers. They examined the wrappers. "It looks like an animal was here," Michelle said. "Did you have this candy in your tent?"

Toby looked down at the ground instead of at Michelle. "It wasn't very much," he said. "I was going to eat it all tonight."

Jared gave a sigh. "The rule about no food is there for a reason. We don't want wild animals coming into the camp. Besides, it's not healthy for them to eat human food. Do you want to make animals sick?"

"No," Toby said in a quiet voice.

"Is that all of it?" Jared asked.

"Yes, I just had one bag."

"All right," Michelle said. "Clean it up, and when you're done, we'll get on with our games."

Jessie leaned down and picked up a wrapper. "We'll help. It won't take as long that way."

There were a lot of wrappers. As the Aldens helped clean them up, Benny said, "Whatever ate all this had to be hungry. This is more candy than I eat on Halloween."

Toby scratched his head. "I don't think one animal could eat all of this. Do you think...do you think it was a bigfoot?"

"Toby, is this another prank?" said Tara. "To try to scare us?"

Toby shook his head. But Violet couldn't tell if he was telling the truth.

"Did you have the tent flap zipped up?" Jessie asked.

"I don't remember. Do you, Henry?"

"Benny and I left before you did," Henry said. "We were already in the bus when you got in."

"I think I zipped it up," Toby said. "But maybe not all the way on the bottom."

"It doesn't matter now," said Jared. "Whatever it was will probably come back, though, since it will think there is more food here." Jared turned to Michelle. "Has this happened before?"

Michelle shook her head. "We had a raccoon visit one year. But not in the daytime. And if it were a bear, the whole tent would have been torn up. I can't imagine what could have done this." Michelle noticed Violet's worried face. She brightened up. "Who's up for some games before bed?"

But for the second night in a row, the children went to bed wondering if there might be something unknown in Bigfoot Valley.

CHAPTER 5

IMPACTFUL CLUES

The next morning Violet was up early. As soon as the first rays of sunlight came through the tent wall, she remembered the night before and couldn't fall back to sleep. She got dressed quietly, put on her shoes, and grabbed her camera. Maybe taking some pictures in the morning sun would get her mind off the strange things going on at Camp Quest.

Violet unzipped the tent flap and was about to step out of the door, but she noticed something in the dirt in front of her. She was so surprised that she took a step back and lost her footing. She fell back almost right on top of her sister.

"What is it?" Jessie said. "It's early."

Violet's voice was trembly. "There are footprints outside our tent. Big ones. Like really big."

"What?" Jessie climbed out of her sleeping bag.

Violet put her foot alongside one of the footprints. Her foot was only about half as long. The footprint was also very wide at the top.

"They're huge," Jessie said, louder than she meant to. She added, "Do you think it's a bear print?"

"What's going on?" said Henry. He rubbed his eyes as he looked out of his tent flap.

Jessie motioned to the footprints. "Come look."

Before long, most of West Camp was awake and outside.

"There are five toe prints," Henry said. "Bears have five toes."

Jared came to the front of the crowd. "I looked up information about bears when I heard I was going to be a counselor here," he said. "You can usually see the claw marks at the ends of the toes in a bear print. These don't have any claw marks. And it's the wrong shape for a bear print. Their feet are wide but not so long. I'm going to go get Dr. Iris. I knew this was a dangerous place to be!"

It didn't take long for Jared to return with Dr. Iris. She knelt down to look at the prints. "Well, this is very interesting," she said.

"She doesn't seem worried," Violet whispered to Jessie. "That's good, right?"

"Right," Jessie said.

"Okay, everyone," Dr. Iris said as she stood back up, "let's do some scientific investigating. What do you think we should do first?"

"Look for more footprints," Henry said. "If a creature was standing in front of the tent, it had to walk here, and it had to walk away."

"Good, that's right," Dr. Iris said. "Nobody move from where you are. We've already been walking around some this morning, so if there are more prints, we may have walked over them, but we should see some traces. Does anyone see another footprint?"

No one did.

"It could have jumped down from the trees and then jumped back," Tara said. Next to the girls' tent, there was a tree with a large branch sticking out.

"I don't think a big creature could jump that far," Jessie said. "Especially to jump back up. A bear couldn't do that."

"A bigfoot might," Toby said. "You don't know how good they are at jumping."

"Let's stick to our investigation of the evidence we have," Dr. Iris said. "What should we do next?"

"Measure them?" Benny said. "Like we're going to measure our fossils."

"And record the measurements," Henry added.

"Right. We need a ruler to measure it and some paper to record it. Michelle, will you go get some supplies from my office?"

When Michelle came back, Dr. Iris handed the ruler to Tara. "Tara, why don't you do the measuring, and,

Jessie, you do the recording. What else do you think we should do?" Dr. Iris asked the rest of the group.

"Draw a picture of them," Violet said.

"Why do we have to draw them?" Toby asked. "Why can't we just take a picture?"

"We could," said Dr. Iris, "but it's a good idea to draw your findings too. What if you are someplace without a phone or a camera, or you have one, but the battery is dead?"

"I'll draw them," Violet said. She wanted to take a picture, but she had agreed not to use her camera when they were doing camp activities. Doing a scientific investigation felt like a camp activity.

"Excellent," Dr. Iris said. "We'll have a good record then."

Tara measured how wide and how long the footprints were, and Jessie wrote down the information.

"We should measure how deep they are too," Henry said.

"That's right," Dr. Iris said. "Part of the depth of a footprint depends on how soft the ground is, and part of it depends on how heavy the animal or person making the footprint is."

"This ground is hard," Henry said, "Our footsteps are barely leaving a mark, but these footprints are deep."

Tara measured. "Two inches deep," she said.

"That's as heavy as a dinosaur!" said Benny.

"Or a very big bigfoot," said Toby.

The group of campers buzzed with chatter about what could have made the prints.

Dr. Iris held up her hand. "I think we need to talk more about Bigfoot—before any of you make what scientists call an *assumption*. Let's meet in the science room after breakfast, and I can talk to all the campers. I know news of these footprints is going to spread. Now why doesn't everyone get dressed? Chef Pepper is expecting you!"

Dr. Iris was right. At breakfast, news about the footprints spread like wildfire through the dining hall. By the time the campers gathered in the science room, people had all kinds of ideas about what might be hiding in the woods.

"I bet it jumped down from the treetops," said one.

"What if it can fly?" asked another.

Dr. Iris quieted everyone down. "I know you've all heard about the unusual footprints and some talk of a bigfoot creature, so let's discuss that. It's a good topic for people interested in science. First, let's talk about what we know. There are stories about creatures like Bigfoot all around the world. Has anyone heard of some of the other names?"

Henry raised his hand. "They call them yetis in the Himalayan mountains."

Dr. Iris nodded. "Yes, there have been reports of unusual footprints and sightings of mysterious creatures in that part of Asia for years. Some mountain climbers who went there came back with those stories. Some of them started using the phrase 'Abominable Snowman' instead of Yeti. And they say that the creature is white, better to blend in with the snowy conditions."

"What does 'abominable' mean?" Tara asked.

"It means something awful," Michelle said.

"Yes," Dr. Iris said, "but some of the people who used that phrase did so because they wanted to make yetis sound scarier, even though they had no proof that yetis even existed. Have any of you heard the phrase 'tall tales'?" Dr. Iris asked.

Most of the older campers had heard the term, but Benny hadn't. "Do bigfoots have big tails too?" he asked.

Dr. Iris smiled. "Tall tales are stories that are told like they are true, but there are parts that are exaggerated, which no one can prove," she said. "After the explorers told their stories, other people retold the stories, even though they hadn't been there. Over time, the stories about yetis changed. They got stranger and scarier."

"I've heard of sasquatches. Are those like bigfoots too?" Violet asked.

"Very good," said Dr. Iris. "'Sasquatch' is a different name for the same sort of creature. In that case, a man heard stories about wild men. The story came from First Nations people in western Canada.

The man had never seen a sasquatch himself, but his were the stories many people read. They became the legend. That is why we call things like sasquatches and yetis and bigfoots creatures of legend."

"So if people have seen yetis in the Himalayas, which are thousands of miles from where people have seen sasquatches, then there really must be bigfoots out there!" Toby said. "The people who saw them all over don't know each other. They all wouldn't be making up the same story."

"That's an interesting point," Dr. Iris said. "If a lot of people report seeing something, does that mean it's true?"

Jessie raised her hand. "There are stories about dragons from a lot of different places in the world, and for a long time people thought they were real, but we know now that dragons don't exist."

"I wish they did!" said Benny. "A real dragon would be almost as cool as a real, live dinosaur."

"I do too!" Dr. Iris said. "But you're right, Benny; they don't exist. Here's one possibility of what might have happened. A long time ago, before there were lots of books, and there were no cameras or television, people relied on reports from travelers about what was out in the world. Imagine you were a traveler from Europe and you went to Africa and saw a giraffe for the first time. That would look like a very strange creature to you! If you wrote a description of a giraffe and drew a picture of it, some people would believe you, but others would think you might have made it up. Sometimes, people like to use their imagination to draw made-up creatures, like dragons and unicorns. Have any of you ever drawn creatures you created in your own imagination?"

"I like to draw birds that have really long tail feathers in all different colors," said Violet. "They look like they could be real birds, but they aren't."

Dr. Iris nodded. "That's what I'm talking about. If someone saw your drawings, they might think you drew something real! So years ago, how was someone supposed to know a unicorn wasn't real but a giraffe was?"

"But that was a long time ago," Toby said. "People are seeing bigfoots now and taking pictures, not just drawing them."

"Yes, there are current reports, but that does not mean they are reliable. Sometimes people set up photographs so something looks real when it isn't. We don't know the truth in the case of these Bigfoot photos and video." Dr. Iris smiled. "It's always good to keep an open mind. Just because you haven't seen something, doesn't mean it doesn't exist. But a scientist would need scientific evidence to say that bigfoots exist. What other kind of evidence do you think we would need?"

"A skeleton or some bones," Henry said. "We know dinosaurs existed because of their bones, even though they died out long before people could see one."

"Like my Monoclonius!" said Benny.

"That's right, Henry," said Dr. Iris. "And, Benny, I'm glad you bring up that particular type of dinosaur. You see, while some scientists believe that the Monoclonius existed, others think that the bones that have been found belong to other, similar species."

Benny frowned. "So Monoclonius wasn't really real?"

Dr. Iris gave Benny a gentle smile. "The truth is, we don't know. We have some evidence, but not enough to say for sure one way or the other. In science, we say that it needs further investigation."

"Like Bigfoot?" said Toby.

Dr. Iris nodded. "A little bit. But unlike Monoclonius, we don't have any bones that we think might be from Bigfoot. Every 'bigfoot' bone has been matched to another creature. No one has found a unique bone—at least not yet."

Violet was surprised that Dr. Iris knew so much about Bigfoot and other creatures of legend. She wondered why she knew so much about them, but before Violet had the chance to ask, Dr. Iris said, "Now let's get to work with our fossils."

The campers took out the fossils they had cleaned up the day before and began to measure and record information.

"Anyone need help?" Dr. Iris asked.

"I have a question." Toby held up one of his fossils. "How do we know these creatures really existed? Why couldn't these just be funny-looking rocks? It could be that someone is making these to fool us, just like you think some of the bigfoot pictures are to fool us."

"Those are good questions, Toby," Dr. Iris said. "If we had only one specimen of these fossils, like this one with the ridges, it might just be a strange rock. But hundreds of thousands of these have been found, and they are all very similar. What could have made rocks look like that? We have tools now to carve rocks, but those tools are very new. People began collecting these fossils many years ago. And so many have been found that it doesn't seem likely that someone is making fake fossils out of rocks to fool people, does it?"

Toby picked up another fossil and held it next to one Henry had found. They looked the exact same. "I guess not," he said.

The campers worked hard all morning on the

fossils. Then at lunch, Dr. Iris announced their afternoon schedule. "After all your hard work, we're going to take a little trip to see what happens when we put lots of little fossils together."

Benny bounced in his seat. "Are we going to see real dinosaurs?" he asked. "Really real ones?"

Dr. Iris smiled. "As real as they get."

CHAPTER 6

THE REAL THING

The campers finished their lunches quickly. Once everyone was on the bus, Michelle began to count to make sure everyone was there.

Jessie looked around. "Where's Tara?" she asked. Jessie had gotten used to looking for her tentmate. Tara seemed to be good at going missing. "Has anyone seen her?"

Toby shook his head.

"She finished lunch before we did," said Violet.

"We thought she had gone ahead of us."

"There she is," Henry said, pointing out the window.

Tara came out from the back of the dining hall and ran to the bus. She was out of breathe when she climbed aboard. "Sorry. I saw Len and wanted to help Chef Pepper unload the supplies."

"That was thoughtful of you," Dr. Iris said. "But we were worried. Remember our buddy system? Let one of your tentmates know where you're going, and try to keep track of the schedule."

"Okay," Tara mumbled as she sat down in front of Violet and Jessie.

Once everyone was seated, the bus began to pull out of the parking lot. Then it screeched to a halt. The delivery van shot in front of them. Len didn't even look their way as he sped off.

"That kid!" the bus driver said. "I wonder where he's off to in such a hurry. He's usually a careful driver."

"Did he say why he was in a rush?" Jessie asked Tara.

"He said he had a lot to do today," Tara said. "I'm

going to take a nap. Wake me up when we get there."

As Tara leaned her head against the window, Jessie and Violet shared a worried look. They had spent more than a day with Tara. She barely seemed interested in talking to them at all. Did she just like time to herself? Or was there another explanation?

After a long ride into town, the bus pulled in to the natural history museum. Inside, the museum was full of dinosaur skeletons, big and small. Right in the middle of the main hall stood a stegosaurus.

"It's even bigger than I thought!" Benny yelled.

As the campers walked around the skeleton, Jessie asked, "Why are some of the bones a different color?"

Their counselor Jared started to answer, but one of the museum staff interrupted him.

"This skeleton is almost complete, but there were a few bones missing," the staffer said. "We made replacement bones out of a special kind of clay. We kept them a different color so you know they aren't part of the original."

"Why would some be missing?" Violet asked.

Again, Jared looked as if he wanted to respond, but the staffer spoke first.

"The soil and temperature conditions have to be just right for bones to fossilize. If a bone doesn't fossilize, it breaks down. That's why you don't find animal bones all over the forest."

"That would be weird to go on a hike and find bones everywhere," Henry said.

"I bet Watch would like that a lot!" said Benny.

Jared stepped in front of the museum staffer. "I'll show you some other interesting fossils," he said. "Follow me." The counselor took them on a tour, telling them all sorts of interesting facts. For the first time since the camp began, Jared seemed excited.

"He's good at this," Violet said to Jessie as they followed him to a display of a winged dinosaur. "It's too bad he couldn't get the job here."

"It is too bad," Jessie said. "It makes me wonder…" She slowed down as Jared led Benny up close to the feet of a Brachiosaurus.

"Is something wrong?" asked Violet.

"I've just been thinking about those footprints back at camp," Jessie said. "Something about them didn't seem right."

"A lot of stuff didn't seem right about them," said Violet. "They were creepy."

"I don't mean that," said Jessie. "It's just that if they were from some creature, there would be other signs."

Henry overheard his sisters and joined them. "I think you're right," he said. "There were just two of them. They seemed a little too perfect."

"Do you think someone might have put them there on purpose?" Jessie asked. "That someone created them to look like bigfoot prints?"

"We know Toby likes to pull pranks," said Violet. "Who else could it be?"

Jessie looked ahead. Jared was now pointing to a different dinosaur and talking excitedly about the spikes on the dinosaur's tail. "Maybe someone who would rather be somewhere else?" she said.

That night, after games around the campfire, everyone went back to their tents. It had been a long day, and the campers had learned a lot. Not only about dinosaurs but about Bigfoot too.

Jessie still didn't believe in Bigfoot. She was sure there was an explanation for the strange things happening at Camp Quest. Still, she couldn't figure out how to make sense of it all.

At last she remembered what Dr. Iris said. The children needed to follow the evidence wherever it led. They did not have enough evidence to follow. With a sigh, Jessie rolled over in her sleeping bag and drifted off to sleep.

Jessie did not expect another clue to come so quickly. Later that night, she awoke with a start. She opened her eyes and listened. She could hear Violet mumbling in her sleep. But no sounds were coming from Tara's sleeping bag. As her eyes adjusted to the dark, Jessie turned so she could look closer.

Her tentmate wasn't there! Jessie sat up. "Tara?" she called softly.

No answer. Just as Jessie was standing up to look outside, the door of the tent zipped open. Tara came back in.

"Is anything wrong?" Jessie asked. "I was worried." Jessie noticed Tara had her phone in her hand.

"I heard noises," Tara said. "Like the first night we were here. A lot of branches breaking and some growling too." She wrapped her arms around herself. "Toby may be right after all. I'm worried there really is a bigfoot out there watching the camp."

"I don't know what's out there, but you probably shouldn't go out alone," Jessie said. "If you hear something else, wake me up, and we can check it out together."

Tara didn't reply to that. "Sorry you were worried," she said and got back in her sleeping bag. Within a few seconds Tara was making sleeping noises. Jessie thought they didn't sound real, but she decided if Tara wanted to pretend she had fallen asleep, she could.

Jessie lay back down. Since she hadn't heard any strange noises herself, she wondered if Tara was telling the truth. Had she gone outside to use her phone?

In the next tent over, Benny hadn't had any trouble falling asleep.

But like Jessie, he too woke up in the night and didn't know why. It was quiet and so dark he knew it was a long time until daylight. There was a bad smell in the air. He realized it smelled a little like the time Watch had gone up to a skunk to make friends, but the skunk had sprayed him. The smell outside the tent wasn't as stinky as that, but it was still bad.

Benny turned over so he was facing the side of the tent. As he was about to close his eyes, he thought he saw a small bit of the tent move, as if someone outside was pushing a hand onto the fabric. A shiver ran through him. He watched, hoping he had imagined it. Since it was right near the bottom of the tent, only a few inches from his face, he knew someone would have to be kneeling down to be pushing at the tent at that spot.

He really didn't want to see the bump again, but he couldn't stop watching. Then he heard a strange noise right where the bump had been. It sounded as if someone was breathing through a stuffy nose. When the side of the tent bumped in again, Benny scooted back and let out a little cry. "Wake up, Henry. There's something outside!"

Toby woke up before Henry. Benny had to shake his brother's shoulder to get him awake. "There's something outside!" Benny said when Henry's eyes opened. "It's trying to get into the tent!"

Toby jumped up, grabbed a flashlight, and ran outside. Henry followed, but Benny was too scared. He could see the light of Toby's flashlight through the side of the tent.

"Shine the light toward the woods," Henry said in a low voice. "I thought I saw some leaves moving."

Benny saw the flashlight beam move away. Then he heard Toby's voice: "Nothing."

"Benny probably just had a bad dream," Henry said. "Come on. Let's get back inside."

When they came back in, Toby made Benny repeat his story three times. "How big was the spot that pushed in? Did it look like fingers?"

"No, it was just one small place."

"What kind of noise was it?" Henry asked.

Benny realized what the noise had reminded him of. "Like the noise Watch makes when he's sniffing for something."

"It might have been Rex," Henry said. "That makes the most sense. Do you think it could have been Rex's nose pushing in on the tent?"

"Maybe," Benny said, "but there was a bad smell too." He'd forgotten about the smell in all the excitement.

"A bad smell? Bigfoots are supposed to smell terrible." Toby's eyes got wide. "Do you think it was the real thing?" He didn't sound as excited as he had before. This time, he sounded a little scared.

"Bigfoot?" said Henry. "Of course not. It was probably just Rex. We'll ask Dr. Iris in the morning if Rex was allowed out. And whatever it was, it's gone now."

"I just hope it stays gone," said Benny.

CHAPTER 7

SMELLY SUSPECT

In the morning, Henry checked the area around the boys' tent. But the ground near the sides of their tent was grassy. He couldn't make out any tracks. "Whatever paid us a visit, it looks like it didn't leave us any clues," he said.

Just then, a shriek came from the direction of the bathroom building. It sounded like Violet. Henry, Jessie, and Benny ran to see what was going on. Toby and Tara followed.

They found Violet on the ground outside of the bathroom building. Next to her, a garbage can had been tipped over. Trash was everywhere.

Henry helped her up. "Are you okay?" he asked.

"I am fine," she said. "Just a little…unclean." She used the grass to wipe off some kind of goo that had gotten on her hand.

Michelle came running up. "What happened? I heard a scream."

"I was on a walk to take some pictures," said Violet. "I guess I wasn't looking and tripped over all this garbage." Violet brushed a brown banana peel off her shoe.

"But how did the garbage get out?" asked Michelle. "The containers are housed in wood boxes to keep the animals away."

Henry thought back to the noises from the night before. "Maybe it was a raccoon," he said. "We heard noises outside our tent last night."

"Smelly noises!" said Benny.

"You did?" asked Tara.

"Well, this is certainly smelly," Michelle said, looking at the remains of the trash bag. "And it does look like some kind of animal has been through it."

"Didn't you say you heard something outside too, Tara?" said Violet.

"I did?" said Tara. "Oh, yes, I did. I went to check it out. It sounded like an animal."

Jessie examined the wooden box that had held the trash bin. The latch that kept it shut hadn't been broken. Someone, or something, had slid it open.

"If an animal did this," said Jessie, "it's a very smart one. One that knows how to open locks."

Michelle looked at Toby. "Did you have anything to do with this?"

"Me?" said Toby, turning red. "If I was going to do a prank—not that I would—it would be fun. It wouldn't have anything to do with garbage."

"Whoever did this, no more pranks," Michelle said. "Violet is being a good sport about it, but I think we've had enough jokes for this camp session.

Now let's get ready for breakfast. I don't know about you, but I'm hungry."

As the girls headed back to their tent to get dressed, something on the edge of the woods caught Violet's eye. The shrubs were dark green, but on one was a bit of light gray. It didn't look like a piece of trash, and it definitely wasn't a flower.

"I see something," she said to the other girls. As she got closer, she could see the bit of gray was actually a clump of dirty white fur.

"What did you find?" Tara said as she and Jessie came up from behind. Toby, Henry, and Benny joined them.

Violet pulled the clump off the shrub. "It's hair or fur snagged on this branch." She wrinkled her nose. "But it smells really bad."

"It might have come from Rex," Henry said. But Henry had to admit the hair looked lighter than Rex's patches of tan fur.

"This didn't come from a bear or a raccoon or Rex," Toby said. "And Benny said it smelled bad. Bigfoots smell bad, so we know what it was. Definitely a bigfoot."

"I thought bigfoots had brown or black hair," Violet said.

"Well...it could be a light-colored one," Toby insisted.

"That's silly," Tara said. "The white ones are the yetis, remember? How would a yeti get here all the way from the Himalayan mountains?"

Tara and Toby began to argue. They were so loud that Benny moved away. As he stood looking into the woods, he thought he saw a blotch of light gray through the underbrush.

As Benny leaned to get a better look, the blob moved a little too. The movement startled Benny, and he almost called out, but he didn't want to scare off the blob. Benny moved farther into the forest. He squinted as his eyes adjusted to the dim light. A bad smell filled Benny's nose—the same smell from the night before.

"Benny, where did you go?" Jessie called.

Just as she did, the creature in the forest began to

move away. Whatever it was, it looked too small to be a bigfoot, but Benny had to be sure. This could be his chance to prove whether Bigfoot was real. He began running through the woods.

"Benny?" called Henry. As soon as Henry saw his little brother running away, he chased after him.

When Henry and the others finally caught up, they found Benny sitting on a log with a new friend. A very smelly new friend.

"I'm going to call him…" Benny thought for a moment as he petted the dog at his feet. "Stinky."

Michelle and Jared caught up. "Careful, Benny," Jared said. "It might be a vicious stray."

But as Benny continued to pet the dog's head, it closed its eyes and thumped its tail on the ground.

"It seems friendly to me," said Benny. "But I think its paw is hurt."

"It's got a collar on," Violet said. She was happy to find out that the mysterious hair had been from a dog, but she didn't want to get any closer. It really did smell. "What can we do with it?"

"I'll go get Dr. Iris," Jessie said. "She'll know what to do."

Jessie ran to the camp director's office and explained what they'd found. When they returned to the campsite, Dr. Iris said, "Just as I figured. This looks like the dog from the newspaper—the one those hikers reported missing."

"So bigfoot wasn't the cause, like Len thought," said Henry.

"No, but I'd say this fellow had a run-in with something. It stinks like skunk." Dr. Iris looked at her watch. "I'll drive it to the veterinarian while everyone is having breakfast. I'm sure the vet's office will either have a copy of the flyer or be able to track down the owner. Poor thing." She gave a little laugh. "Poor me. My car is going to smell awful after this. But it can't be helped. Come along, fellow."

The dog obeyed, following after her and wagging its tail.

"At least we know what ate the candy bars," Henry said. "The dog probably smelled them and slipped in through the crease in the flap."

"It must have been looking for more food last night," said Benny. "That's why it got into the trash."

"The owner will be really glad we found the dog. Good job, Benny," Violet said.

"And all before breakfast!" Henry said with a chuckle.

The children cleaned up and headed toward the dining hall. "I've been thinking," Jessie said. "That dog might have found the trash, but it didn't open the latch to get the food out."

"Maybe it was unlatched," said Violet. "Like the way the boys forgot to zip up their tent and let the dog get their candy."

"Maybe..." said Jessie. It seemed like a big coincidence.

"One thing's for sure," said Henry. "The dog did *not* leave those big tracks outside your tent. We still don't know who—or what—did that."

The children walked in silence for a little bit, then Henry noticed something glimmering on the side of the path. He knelt down and picked it up out of the underbrush. "It looks like a serving spoon from the dining hall."

"Why would a serving spoon be all the way out here?" Violet asked.

"Maybe Stinky was using it to eat his supper last night," Benny joked.

Henry held it up in the sunlight. "It hasn't been here long. Let's take it to Chef Pepper. He might know if he's missing one."

The children headed to the kitchen, and the chef was surprised to see them. "What are you doing with one of my spoons?" he asked Jessie.

"We found it," Jessie said, handing it to him.

"Covered up with dirt by the edge of the trail," Violet added.

"You didn't lend out a spoon to anyone, did you?" Henry asked.

"No. No one has ever asked to borrow a big spoon like this. That would be a strange request!"

"Are you sure it's a camp spoon?" Jessie said.

"I'm sure. They all come from the same company." The chef turned over the spoon and pointed at some tiny letters etched into the back of the handle. "But I can check my inventory list to be sure." He went over to the corner of the kitchen where there was a desk and a file cabinet. He got a file out of the cabinet.

"Why don't one of you count the spoons in those holders there," he said, pointing to two canisters full of large spoons.

"Twenty-nine," Violet said when she was done counting. "And the one we found is bent up compared to these other ones."

Chef Pepper looked up from the file. "There are supposed to be thirty. I make sure we have the right number of kitchen utensils at the start of every camp season. So this *is* one of our spoons. Why would someone want this?"

"I don't know," said Jessie. "But I have a feeling there is still more to this mystery than a shaggy dog."

TRACES

Michelle had just finished counting everyone on the bus when Dr. Iris's car pulled into the parking lot. The camp director hurried over and came up the steps. "I'm not going with you today, but I thought West campers would like an update on the dog they found. The vet knows the dog's owner and has already called him. It looks like the dog is not badly hurt. He just needed some healthy food and medicine and a bandage for his paw."

"And a bath!" Benny called.

"And a bath." Dr. Iris laughed. "Okay, you can be off on your expedition. Michelle is in charge. See you later."

The bus took them to another spot in the stream to hunt fossils. Here they found even more than they had the day before. It was another hot day, and Jared stayed in the shade by the cooler.

Tara and Toby were still competing to see who could find the most. "Move farther away, Toby," Tara ordered. "You don't have to look in the same spots I do." She reached down and picked up a very smooth rock shaped like a triangle. "What is this? I don't remember something like this on the charts, but it looks like it is a fossil."

Michelle hurried over and examined it. "Wow! What a find! I think this is a shark tooth from a prehistoric species of white shark called a *Carcharias*. It's not on the charts because it's so unusual to find one here."

Benny looked around. "How did a shark tooth

get here?" he asked. "Sharks live in the ocean."

"Yes," Michelle said. "And millions of years ago, this area was covered by a warm, shallow ocean called the Western Interior Seaway. So sharks did live here then. The earth then did not look like the earth now. Very nice find, Tara."

"I would have found that if Tara had let me look by her!" Toby said. He stomped away down the stream, splashing water everywhere.

"You two! Remember, we talked about cooperation," Michelle said.

"I found something else that isn't on the charts," Henry called. "It's like a leaf print etched on the rock."

"Another good find!" Michelle exclaimed when she went over to look at it. "This is something called a trace fossil. Trace fossils are animal footprints or the mark of a leaf that left an impression before it decayed. Not only animals but also plants have changed over time. Many plant species that existed in prehistoric times can't be found now. It looks like this is a partial print, so I don't know what kind of plant this is. We'll have to research it. But we're having such a good day!"

Toby turned from where he had stomped off upstream. "Guys!" he called. "I just saw something moving in the woods! Something big!"

All the campers hurried to the spot where he stood.

"I don't see anything," Henry said, shading his eyes with his hand while he looked up into the woods.

"I don't either," Jessie said.

"It was there. I know I saw it," Toby insisted.

"It could have been a deer," Michelle said. "Remember, animals in the woods are more scared of us than we are of them."

"Not something ten feet tall!" Toby said.

"It could have been a bear. We should go back to camp," Jared urged. "Whatever it was, it's too close to us. It's time to go back anyway."

"You're right about the time," Michelle said. "Okay, everyone, collect your things," she called.

Once the campers had cleaned up the site, Henry and Jessie went to see if Michelle and Jared needed help with the cooler and the other camp supplies. As they got close, they overheard Michelle say to Jared, "You know bears won't bother us as long as we don't bother them. You're going to make some of the campers scared to be here."

"No one but me seems to think of what dangers could be out there!" Jared shot back.

Michelle noticed Henry and Jessie. "We'll talk about it later," she said to Jared.

Once they were all back at camp, Michelle came to speak with Jessie and Henry. "I hope you aren't scared by anything Jared said. The camp has always been safe."

"We're not scared," Jessie said. "Violet and I know that Jared doesn't like it here. He told us about the other job he wanted."

"Yes, it's too bad he couldn't get that job. I knew he'd never been camping before, but I didn't think he'd be so unhappy," Michelle said. "Please tell me if some of the younger campers seem scared by what happened today."

"We will," Henry said. "I'm not sure Toby actually saw anything. He really, really wants to see a bigfoot, so he may have imagined it."

"Yes, that's true," Michelle said. "He's certainly interested in Bigfoot. Let's hope if there is something out there, it won't bother us tonight! I'd like a quiet night. I'm ready for dinner and then a little bit of stargazing and then my nice sleeping bag!"

—

The evening did pass quietly, and Jessie woke up the next morning feeling rested. But there was something strange about the tent. She felt sun on her face. Why was the sun so bright? Had she overslept?

She could also feel a breeze on her face. When she sat up and rubbed her eyes, she saw where the sun was coming in, but she couldn't believe what she was seeing. There were four big slashes in the side of the tent.

Violet mumbled, "Is it morning?"

"Yes, Violet. Wake up," Jessie told her.

"What is it? Your voice sounds weird."

Violet sat up too, and Jessie pointed at the cuts in the tent. She felt herself shivering, even though it wasn't cold.

"Who would do that?" Violet asked.

"I don't know. It looks like an animal clawed the tent." Jessie took a couple of deep breaths, trying to stay calm. "At least whatever did it isn't out there now. I don't hear anything. Do you?"

"No." Then Violet grabbed Jessie's arm. "Where's Tara?"

Tara's sleeping bag was empty. The two girls scrambled up. Jessie was first through the flap, but she stopped so suddenly that Violet bumped into her.

"The footprints are back," Violet said, peering around her sister. "And there are lots more of them." Several footprints led to the tent and away from it.

"We can't stay in here. We have to get a counselor, and we have to find Tara," Jessie said. "I'll go first. I'm going to step out to the side so I don't step on

the footprints. Try to do the same."

Once they were outside, the girls ran to Michelle's tent and called her name.

She was already awake and had just finished getting dressed. "What is it? You sound scared," the counselor said as she came out of the tent.

Violet took hold of Michelle's hand and pulled her in the direction of their tent. "We don't know where Tara is, and you have to see."

"There are slashes in the side of our tent," Jessie added. She looked around, hoping Tara had just gotten up early, but she didn't see her.

Other campers and Jared came out of their own tents to join them.

"Has anyone seen Tara?" Michelle asked. No one answered.

"Tara!" Toby called out. He looked scared.

"This is very serious," Jared said. "I'm going to get Dr. Iris."

"Did a creature take Tara away?" one of the younger campers asked and then began to cry.

"What's going on?" a girl's voice came from the path.

"Tara!" Violet exclaimed. Jessie and Violet ran up and hugged her.

"We were so worried," Jessie said.

"Where have you been?" Michelle asked. "What did I say about the buddy system?"

"I was taking a shower." She pointed to her wet hair. "I woke up early and couldn't go back to sleep, so I thought I'd wash my hair. What is everyone looking at?"

They took her over to the footprints and showed her the slashes in the tent. While everyone was talking, Jessie whispered to Tara, "Would Toby do something like this to try to scare you? He seemed mad at you because you found the shark tooth."

"No. Toby wouldn't do this. His pranks are silly," Tara said. "I'm starting to think there really are bigfoots hanging around here. It's time for Dr. Iris to let those of us who are scared go home."

Dr. Iris and Jared came hurrying down the path.

When she saw the cuts in the tent, Dr. Iris's face took on a very stern look. She called for everyone to gather round.

"This is no prank," she said. "Someone has damaged camp property on purpose, and that is very serious. Now I want whoever did this to admit what they've done."

No one said anything.

Finally, Tara spoke up. "You have to call my parents," she said. "There is an awful creature out there. Toby can stay if he wants, but I want to go home." Many other campers began to talk, asking Dr. Iris to call their parents too.

"We are not going to let panic take over," Dr. Iris said. "I want everyone to get dressed and go to the dining hall for breakfast. I'll talk to the whole camp then. Counselors, some of the younger children may need a little extra help getting ready this morning. I'll see you in a few minutes." She headed back to her office.

Henry moved over to the side of the tent. "If it

really was a creature, why aren't there any footprints next to the place where the cuts in the tent were made? The footprints just go in a circle. They start by Jared's tent and end in the same place."

"Yes! Remember what Michelle said about trace fossils?" Jessie said. "We should see at least some partial footprints in other places. These are all exactly the same."

"That's right," Violet said. "Maybe it really is someone playing a prank."

"I don't want to stay out here anymore," Benny said. "Can we get dressed and go to the dining hall?"

"Yes, let's do that," Jessie said. Then as the girls were getting ready in their tent, she asked, "Tara, did you notice these tears in the wall when you woke up to go shower?"

Tara shrugged. "I guess I didn't notice it. It was early. The sun was just starting to shine."

Jessie looked at the light streaming through the wall of the tent. It seemed like it would be hard not to notice. And why was Tara getting up so early?

Tara stood up from her cot. "They'll have to send us home now," she said.

"I don't want to go home," Violet said. "If it really was a creature, wouldn't we have heard something? Why would something sneak up, make the slashes, and then go away?"

Tara scowled. "I don't know, but I don't want to be here another night."

Jessie noticed it had gotten darker in the tent. She went back to the door just as a loud clap of thunder sounded and rain began to fall. She sighed. "I don't think we are going to be able to hunt fossils today."

"Hey, Tara, I'll race you!" Toby called from the doorway of the other tent.

Tara got her phone out of her duffel bag and put it in her pocket. She pushed past Jessie. "You're on," she shouted.

Something fluttered to the ground as she took off running toward the dining hall. "Tara, you dropped something!" Violet yelled, but Toby was shouting at the same time, and Tara kept running.

Jessie grabbed the piece of paper and brought it inside.

"Oh, it's just the camp map," she said, pointing at the rectangle on the map that represented the main lodge. "Tara put a bunch of *X*'s inside the building. We didn't have any of those rooms on the scavenger hunt."

Violet leaned in to see. "She put an *X* in this little box off the kitchen. Isn't that the storage room?"

"Yes!" Jessie said. "I guess all those times she kept disappearing during the scavenger hunt, she was exploring inside the lodge, but I don't know what was so interesting."

Henry's voice came from outside the tent. "Michelle brought a tarp to put over your tent," he said. "Come help us put it up."

Jessie put the map in her pocket. She was starting to understand why Tara kept disappearing, but she still had questions. As soon as they were done putting up the tarp, she was going to get more answers.

FOLLOWING THE
EVIDENCE

The Aldens made it to the dining hall just before the rain began to pour. Inside, word had spread quickly of the slashes in the tent and the strange footprints outside. The Aldens found Tara seated at a table surrounded by campers from the other campsites. Jessie knew she'd have to wait to talk to her.

Dr. Iris stood up and called for everyone's attention. "I know most of you have heard what happened in West Camp this morning. This was a very serious incident. When someone damages property, it is not a prank."

A camper raised their hand. "How do you know it was a prank? We heard it was a creature that slashed through the tent."

Everyone began talking again, and Dr. Iris had to raise her hand to get people to quiet down.

"We don't have enough evidence to know that, and the lack of footprints next to the tent lead me to believe it wasn't," she said. "However, no matter what it was, I'm very sorry this camp session has been so upsetting for some of you. It makes me upset. Camp Quest was supposed to be a wonderful experience that you'd always remember. I am going to spend the morning considering whether or not we will end this camp session early." She sighed and looked toward the windows.

"Since the forecast is for thunderstorms all day, we will be staying at camp. We'll do our rain schedule: art, science, and free time for each camp group. During the free time, you can get a game out of the game closet and bring it to the dining hall, or you can get a book to read from the library shelf or one you brought from home. I'll be in my office. I encourage whoever damaged the tent to come talk to me."

West campers had the first free time, but when Jessie looked around for Tara, she didn't see her anywhere. The Aldens gathered at one of the tables in the corner of the dining hall.

"What should we do?" Benny asked.

"I don't know," Violet said. "It's hard to concentrate on anything. I wish we knew who did that to our tent."

"Let's go over what we know," said Henry. "I'll start. We know that the dog that Benny found explains some things, like the smelly visitor at night and the patch of fur. But we don't know who is pulling the bigfoot pranks."

"Toby seems to like being the center of attention," said Violet. "I think he is a suspect."

"That's true. But we can't forget about Tara,"

said Jessie. "She keeps disappearing. She's been up to something. But I'm not sure what yet."

"I wonder about Jared," said Henry. "It's clear he doesn't want to be here. Do you think he might be trying to get the camp to end early?"

Jessie wrote down those names on a piece of paper. "I think those are our suspects," she said. "Then there was that spoon we found soon after the tracks appeared."

Violet took out her sketchbook to look at the image she drew of the footprints. "They were so deep," she said. "Whatever made them would have to be really, super heavy."

"Or," said Jessie. "What if they weren't pressed down at all. What if someone just wanted to make them look like the real thing?"

Henry picked up on where Jessie was going. "They would need a tool—just the right size to make it look realistic."

"The spoon!" said Violet.

"We need to see if another spoon is missing,"

Henry said. "And figure out how someone made those slashes in the tent. It had to be a knife or a pair of scissors. Let's talk to Chef Pepper."

In the kitchen, the chef was reading a newspaper and shaking his head.

"We came to see if you are missing another spoon," Violet said.

"I am! I'm missing a spoon and one pair of my kitchen shears. I only have two pairs of shears, and I have to say, I am not happy about this. I could overlook someone borrowing a spoon, but to do it more than once and take a pair of kitchen shears is quite serious."

He laid down the newspaper on one of the counters and pointed to the headline. "And there is something even more upsetting." The headline read, "Mysterious Footprints at Local Camp. Bigfoot?" Right underneath was a photograph of one of the footprints.

"This is bad news," the chef said. "Len must have gotten this story from someone here, but I don't know how. I'm worried other newspapers and websites will pick up the story. And that means we'll be getting calls from journalists and from parents worried about the safety of their children. The story is bad enough, but the photograph makes it worse. I don't know who would have taken that and shared it."

"Aren't the counselors allowed to have phones?" Jessie asked. "Tara said Jared had his, so he or one of the others could have taken the picture."

"The counselors are only supposed to use theirs at night in their tents," the chef said. "If Tara saw Jared using his, he was breaking the rules."

Two of the counselors came to the door and called to the chef, and he went over to talk to them.

"Tara has a phone too," Violet said.

"She does?" Henry said. "How do you know?"

"We saw it the first night," Violet replied. "She brought it to camp because she is playing a computer game and she has to log into it each day. That's why she doesn't want to be at camp."

Jessie thought about what had bothered her the first night of camp. She also remembered the X's on

Tara's map. "If Tara has been using her phone every day, then she has to charge it somewhere. I think I might know where to find her."

Jessie walked over to the storage room and opened the door. Inside, Tara was sitting on a crate and looking at her phone, which was plugged into an outlet.

When the door opened, she stood up in surprise, and a pair of kitchen shears dropped from her backpack.

"Tara, did you put the cuts in the tent?" Violet asked.

"And make the footprints to scare people?" Jessie added.

Tara gave a big sigh and pulled out the spoon from her bag. "I guess it doesn't make sense to lie now," she said. "I wasn't going to keep them," she said. "I was waiting until the chef left the kitchen to put them back." She looked up at them. "I'm sorry! I feel terrible about it now. I didn't think Dr. Iris would get so upset and talk about closing the whole camp. I just thought she'd let the campers who wanted to leave go home early."

"You have to tell her it was you," Violet said.

"She'll be really angry," Tara said as she got up. She started to cry.

Jessie put her arm around her tentmate. "It will be better if you tell her than if she finds out some other way."

Tara wiped her eyes. "I know. Okay, I'll tell her. Will you go with me to her office?"

When they got to the door of Dr. Iris's office, the camp director was talking on the phone. "We may have to shut camp early," they heard her say. "The nurse just told me she's had several children come to her with stomach upsets and hives and headaches, all of which she thinks are because they are so upset. I'm not going to force children who are miserable to stay at camp. I'm afraid no one will want to send their children here again."

Tara sniffled from the doorway, and Dr. Iris looked up. "I'll call you back," she said and hung up the phone. "Tara, what's wrong?"

Tara didn't say anything. She glanced over her

shoulder at Jessie. "It's okay," Jessie said. Tara nodded and walked into the camp director's office, shutting the door behind her.

The Aldens walked back to the dining room and sat down at a table.

"That solves some of the biggest mysteries," Henry said. "But we still don't know what made the noises in the woods the first night. The noises didn't come from a dog, and I don't think a bear could make that noise."

"If it was a person, they'd have to be making those scary noises on purpose," Jessie said.

"What person?" Violet asked. "That doesn't sound like a fun thing to do."

"What about Jared?" Henry suggested. "He wasn't with us at the campfire."

"I doubt it," said Jessie. "Jared doesn't seem to want to be outside any longer than he has to."

The Aldens walked to where Jared sat staring out at the rain. He looked sad.

"Jared," Henry said. "We are trying to figure out

who ran through the woods and made the noises in the woods the first night of camp. You weren't playing a prank on us, were you?"

"Me?" said Jared. "Go into the woods alone at night? No way! I really did have a terrible headache."

"So you weren't trying to get camp canceled?" asked Jessie.

Jared shook his head. "I know I haven't been a very good counselor this week, and I'm sorry about that. I was just so upset about not getting the job at the museum. But I shouldn't have let that hurt your experience. If camp does continue, I'm going to do my best to make things better."

The Aldens thanked Jared and went back to their table.

"So if nobody was playing a prank that first night," said Violet, "then what was making those noises?"

Henry sighed. "I guess that's one mystery we can't solve on this trip."

"So it really could have been a bigfoot?" Benny asked.

Jessie thought back to what Dr. Iris had told them in the science room, about when there was not enough evidence to know something for certain. In her notebook, next to the description of the strange sounds from that first night, she wrote, "Needs Further Investigation."

CHAPTER 10

A NEW ADVENTURE

When Tara finally came out of Dr. Iris's office, her face was streaked with tears, but she was smiling.

"The camp isn't going to close down, and I get to stay," she announced. "Dr. Iris called my parents." The smile disappeared from her face. "They were really, really mad. I'm going to be grounded when I go home, and I won't be able to play my game for a month. They wanted to come get me today, but

Dr. Iris actually convinced them to let me stay. She figured out a way I can make up for the damage to the tent."

"How?" Jessie asked.

"I'm going to stay for a few extra days after camp ends to help. I'll be helping to clean and to paint some of the buildings. My parents are coming to pick up Toby, and then they'll check into a hotel in town to wait for me to be done."

She looked anxiously at the Aldens. "You'll still be my friends, won't you?"

"Yes," Violet said. "But no more pranks."

That got Jessie thinking. "We thought the spider prank was Toby. Was that you too?"

Tara shook her head. "No, that was Toby. I got him to admit it. He thought he was smart by putting all the spiders in his own tent. It gave me the idea to start doing a prank of my own."

"What about the garbage bin?" asked Jessie. "There was no way that dog got into it on his own."

Tara nodded. "I had spread the trash around to

119

make it look like an animal did it. But I didn't think a real animal would show up! That spooked me out."

"You and the rest of us!" said Violet.

"Well, I have a feeling the only creatures we'll be seeing the rest of the week will be from millions of years ago," said Tara.

The rest of the week went by without any big surprises, except for the one that came on the last day. Grandfather arrived at the same time as Tara and Toby's father.

"You'll have to write to us," Jessie told Tara.

"I will," Tara said. "And if you come back next summer, we can be tentmates again."

"You want to come back?" Violet said.

"Now I do. There are lots more fossils to find!"

"I'm coming back too," Toby said. "But I'm glad camp is done for this year. We get to go stay at a hotel with a giant swimming pool while we're waiting for Tara. And we're going hiking to Bigfoot Ridge." He pulled a piece of paper out of his pocket and unfolded it. It was the map he'd had on the first day. "Tara may have found a shark tooth, but I'm going to find a bigfoot!"

"Maybe you'll find a bigfoot," Tara said. "And maybe not. But while you are off looking for it, I'm going to get good at painting—better than you."

The Aldens laughed at the competitive siblings.

"I see you have gotten to know my children very well," Toby and Tara's father said. "At least you won't both be doing the same thing at the same time," their father said. "Fewer arguments that way."

"Good luck!" Henry said to Toby. "Let us know what you find."

"I will," Toby called as he climbed in his father's van.

"I'd like to say good-bye to Iris before we leave," Grandfather said.

"There she is," Benny said. Dr. Iris and Rex were walking toward them.

"Could I talk to you all in my office?" the camp director asked when she reached them. She sounded serious. Violet got a little nervous as they followed her into the building. She hoped they hadn't done anything wrong.

When they went into the office, Dr. Iris said, "Please relax, everyone." She smiled at Grandfather. "I'm so happy I've had a chance to get to know you all this week. It's been a very unusual camp session!" She explained about the footprints and the slashes in the tent. "But your grandchildren didn't get upset. They didn't jump to conclusions about what was happening. They were such a big help that I have a proposal to make."

"A proposal?" Benny asked. "Isn't that when someone asks someone else to marry them?"

Dr. Iris laughed. "That's one kind of proposal. I have a different kind. I'm doing quite a bit of traveling over the next month after we close up the camp. You probably noticed that what I've been searching for this week hasn't been fossils. I've been looking for other things—a kind of side project."

"What kind of side project?" said Violet.

"Well, as you know I am a paleontologist. But one

thing that brought me to this location was the rumors of Bigfoot. It's something I do on the side, a hobby. I research unexplained mysteries, similar to things like Bigfoot."

"Creatures of legend," said Henry, remembering the term she had used in the science room.

"That's right. I hope to use my research for a new television show I've been asked to put together. It's a program for children investigating the unknown."

"That sounds awesome!" said Benny.

"I'm glad you think so," said Dr. Iris. "That leads me to what I wanted to ask you. You see, I realized I could use some young people to help me know what to include. And I'd love for you Aldens to travel with me."

Violet bounced up and down in excitement.

"Can we, Grandfather?" Henry asked. "School doesn't start for two more months."

Grandfather smiled. "Yes, Dr. Iris has already told me about her plans. The question is, are you all up for another mystery?"

The children all agreed. They couldn't think of anything better than a summer full of mysteries—even if they were a little spooky sometimes.

"Yes!" they said together.

"Excellent," said Dr. Iris. "We leave in one week. That should give you some time to get ready. I have to warn you, though, our next stop is much colder than Colorado, even in the summertime. Make sure to pack some warm clothes!"

Read on for a sneak preview of

MYSTERY OF THE HIDDEN ELVES

the second book in the all-new
Boxcar Children Creatures of
Legend series!

"Land ho!" Benny Alden called, pointing out the window of the airplane. For hours, he had seen only the white waves of the ocean far below. Now, as he pressed his nose up to the window, a green island rose up in the distance.

"It just comes right up out of the water," Jessie said, peering past her brother.

Violet had been napping in the row behind Benny and Jessie. She rubbed her eyes. "It's so green. I thought Iceland would be more…icy."

Henry looked up from the guidebook he was reading. "Greenland is the icier one. It's even farther north than Iceland."

Benny tilted his head. "So Greenland is icier, and Iceland is greener? That's confusing."

Henry laughed. "I agree. But Iceland can get icy too, especially in the winter."

"Well, it's a good thing we're visiting in the middle of the summer," Violet said. "I hope we get perfect weather. I want to take lots of pictures."

The pilot came over the speaker to announce

they were starting their descent. As the plane turned, the children got an even better view of the coast. In the distance, they could see white-tipped mountains. It had been a long flight, but their destination was already worth the wait.

Then something caught Jessie's eye. At first she thought it was a storm cloud over the mountains. But when they got closer, she saw that it looked more like smoke. Jessie liked to be prepared when she and her brothers and sister traveled. "Excuse me," she said as a flight attendant walked past, checking seat belts. "Is there a wildfire going on?"

The flight attendant shook her head and spoke calmly. "The smoke you see is coming from a volcano. Iceland has about thirty active volcanoes."

"Thirty!" Benny stuck his nose up to the window. "Is there hot lava everywhere?"

Violet did not like the sound of that.

The flight attendant gave a gentle smile. "No need to worry. With so many volcanoes, we get some activity about every five years, but it is not like the pictures you see of hot lava and fire."

"I'd like to see a volcano close up someday," Jessie said. "Just not this trip."

"So they aren't dangerous?" Violet asked.

"The biggest danger is from ashfall," the flight attendant said. "It can make it hard to breathe, and if the heat melts the ice, then we worry about flooding. But we have many scientists who monitor them. They'll tell us when we need to be more careful." She smiled. "We're almost ready to land. Please stay in your seats until all the other passengers get off. I will take you to meet someone who will take you to meet your party."

After the flight attendant left, Violet said, "If that volcano erupts, the scientists who are watching it can't stop it."

"Dr. Iris will tell us if it's a problem," said Henry. Dr. Iris was a friend of Grandfather's. She was a paleontologist, but she also had another job: investigating unsolved mysteries around the world. She was planning a television program for children about the mysteries.

Jessie got out a small journal. "I'm going to write down that we saw a volcano. Dr. Iris said she wants to know everything that interests us, so she knows what to talk about when she films the program."

"I hope this trip doesn't have as many scary things happen as the last time we were with Dr. Iris," Violet said. She loved going on adventures and traveling. But sometimes the legends of creatures worried her, even if she was pretty sure they weren't real.

Benny did not seem worried at all. He bounced up and down in his seat. "I see the airport! We're almost there!"

Check out The Boxcar Children® Interactive Mysteries!

Have you ever wanted to help the Aldens crack a case? Now you can with these interactive, choose-your-own-path-style mysteries!

978-0-8075-2850-1 · US $6.99

978-0-8075-2860-0 · US $6.99

978-0-8075-2862-4 · US $6.99

**Henry, Jessie, Violet, and Benny Alden
are on a secret mission that takes
them around the world!**

When Violet finds a turtle statue that nobody's seen
before in an old trunk at home, the children are on the
case! The clue turns out to be an invitation to the
Reddimus Society, a secret guild dedicated to returning
lost treasures to where they belong.

Now the Aldens must take the statue and six mysterious
boxes across the country to deliver them safely—and keep
them out of the hands of the Reddimus Society's enemies.
It's just the beginning of
the Boxcar Children's
most amazing
adventure yet!

JOURNEY ON A RUNAWAY TRAIN
Created by Gertrude Chandler Warner

HC 978-0-8075-0695-0
PB 978-0-8075-0696-7

THE CLUE IN THE PAPYRUS SCROLL
Created by Gertrude Chandler Warner

HC 978-0-8075-0698-1
PB 978-0-8075-0699-8

THE DETOUR OF THE ELEPHANTS
Created by Gertrude Chandler Warner

HC 978-0-8075-0684-4
PB 978-0-8075-0685-1

THE SHACKLETON SABOTAGE
Created by Gertrude Chandler Warner

HC 978-0-8075-0687-5
PB 978-0-8075-0688-2

THE KHIPU AND THE FINAL KEY
Created by Gertrude Chandler Warner

HC 978-0-8075-0681-3
PB 978-0-8075-0682-0

THE COMPLETE FIVE-BOOK MINISERIES
Created by Gertrude Chandler Warner

Also available as a boxed set!
978-0-8075-0693-6 · $34.95

Add to Your
Boxcar Children Collection!

The first sixteen books are now available in
four individual boxed sets!

978-0-8075-0854-1 · US $24.99   978-0-8075-0857-2 · US $24.99   978-0-8075-0840-4 · US $24.99   978-0-8075-0834-3 · US $24.99

The Boxcar Children® Bookshelf includes the first twelve
books, a bookmark with complete title checklist,
and a poster with activities.

978-0-8075-0855-8 · US $69.99

THE BOXCAR CHILDREN® MYSTERIES

GERTRUDE CHANDLER WARNER discovered when she was teaching that many readers who like an exciting story could find no books that were both easy and fun to read. She decided to try to meet this need, and her first book, *The Boxcar Children*, quickly proved she had succeeded.

Miss Warner drew on her own experiences to write the mystery. As a child she spent hours watching trains go by on the tracks opposite her family home. She often dreamed about what it would be like to set up housekeeping in a caboose or freight car—the situation the Alden children find themselves in.

While the mystery element is central to each of Miss Warner's books, she never thought of them as strictly juvenile mysteries. She liked to stress the Aldens' independence and resourcefulness and their solid New England devotion to using up and making do. The Aldens go about most of their adventures with as little adult supervision as possible—something else that delights young readers.

Miss Warner lived in Putnam, Connecticut, until her death in 1979. During her lifetime, she received hundreds of letters from girls and boys telling her how much they liked her books.